Savage Space Salvage

Eric Kercher

Paper and Sword, LLC

For Noah

From the Author

There are days when we all need an escape from a terrible job, a terrible day, or a terrible life.

Join my newsletter and get an escape from the real world, stories, and lore designed to entertain and delight.

You'll also get *Stories from the Deep*, an exclusive, unpublished anthology chock full of extra epilogues, short stories, and lore from the Patmos Sea Fantasy Adventure Series.

Join now at erickercher.com.

Enjoy the book.

-Eric Kercher

Savage Space Salvage

Stars twinkled out the front visor, flashing in the nebula of pain. Stella sat watching it, a cooling cup of fragrant, steaming coffee languishing in her hands.

"Trouble sleeping?"

She turned. Dave stood in the hatch, silhouetted by the cool, blue light of the corridor behind.

"Some." She returned to her staring, the hard chair holding her. Dave joined her, taking the pilot's seat next to her.

They sat in silence for a while, then finally Stella licked her lips. "Are we doing the right thing?"

"I think so. What else would happen to it? Drift forever, unused?"

"You make it sound noble."

"In a way, it is. We re-purpose what has been lost."

Stella shivered and rubbed her arms with her hands. The ship was warm, but not enough to cover the chill that ran down her back.

"Today was a hard day, I know that." He reached over and patted her knee. "You're going to be fine. Eventually, this will fade, and the next job will come up."

She turned away. "I just can't..." Memories flashed through her mind. She wiped one eye, then the other.

"Death is the one thing we can count on," Dave said. She didn't turn back, and he eventually stood. "Goodnight, Stella, wake me if you need anything."

He left her to her thoughts. Stella stayed on the bridge until her coffee stopped steaming, then turned cold, hugging herself.

"Message incoming," the ship said, a soft, female tone that inspired confidence and soothed nerves.

"Send it to me," Dave said. He picked up his tablet, reading it as it streamed in. A half-smile appeared on his face. "Sandy, tell the crew to gather. We've got another job."

He walked down to the dining space, the sounds of the ship talking to the other distant. The smell of breakfast lingered in the air—re-hydrated potatoes and proteins. He poured a cup of coffee as the others came in.

"What's up?" Sal said, picking a reconstituted orange from the fruit bowl and peeling it. "Another job?"

"You know it."

Sal smiled, then clenched a fist. "Hot dog, I'm in for a mile."

"We'll cover the details when everyone else gets in."

They chatted, making small talk, as the others joined. Sally, Zeld, and then finally Stella.

She had dark bags under her eyes, and took a seat without saying anything.

"I'll cut to the chase," Dave said. He flicked up on his tablet, and the hologram of space appeared above the table. "We've got a tip on the Orion network about a missing freighter loaded with synthesized proteins."

The computer zoomed in on a section of space, highlighting a track that circled through empty space, then disappeared. "Rescue crews combed the area, but couldn't pick up the ship's signature."

The ship in question appeared, turning slowly. *Independence* was splashed underneath it in bright, white letters.

Stella retreated, which Dave noticed. "She had a crew of three, all presumed dead. If we can get to it before the proteins go bad, that food will do a lot of good to the Cyclosian colonies less than a parsec away. The freight company has already written it off as a loss and it's eligible for salvage."

"So we just have to find it, that's it?" Sal asked.

"That's it. I've already altered course, and we'll be in the sector in a few days."

"They didn't find it during the search?" Zeld asked.

"No trace. We've got the search area here." A section of space glowed red. "They had two rescue ships with long-range scanners try the most likely areas of breakdowns."

"What about attacks?" Stella asked, breaking her silence.

Dave paused. "The freight company never got a distress call. The crew checked in as normal and then went silent. There could have been an attack, for all we know, but they never told anyone about it if they did."

"They might not have had the time," Sal said. "Pirates move fast."

"Unlikely," Dave said. "Low-cost freight, too much risk. There are easier, higher-paying targets out there in space. My guess is a malfunction that took out the communication equipment at the same time."

"And all the backups?" Stella asked.

Dave shrugged. "It's been known to happen. Zeld, Sal, do the research on the ship. Everyone else, you know what to do."

Cool, steady air from the ventilation blew down on Dave. Even though it was filtered air, it still smelled like fresh air. The others left, going to their respective tasks, but Stella remained.

"This is my last job," she said after they were alone. Dave's frown tightened. "I'd like to get off when we get to Sirus."

"I respect that, and even though I'm disappointed by it, I think I understand."

"I'm not cut out for this, Dave." Her hand trembled.

"Stella, I've known you for years. You're stronger than you think you are."

She turned her head, away from him.

"Please look at me." She did, her green eyes locking onto his, studying his face, examining him. "Is this about what... Is this about us?"

She looked away. "No."

He approached her, knelt down. "If it is, I'm sorry, and we'll never do it again."

"Dave, it isn't that. I've made my decision. Please let me make it."

He nodded, got back to his feet, then turned away from her. "I'll make the arrangements at the next dock." His voice was ice-cold, as cold as the space that surrounded them. "I'll be on the bridge if you need me."

He left her, dwelling on his own thoughts, and tried to keep his emotions in check.

Stella worked methodically. She didn't feel the food beneath her fingers, or the tools she used to prepare it. Her mind was on other things.

Disturbing things.

The knife clicked as she cut up the protein, striking the cutting board. She finished it and dumped it into the cooker. It steamed and released its aroma, almost as close to real beef as you could get out here.

There was some comfort in her actions, and comfort in the dish she was making. She thought it would dispel the memories, make them go away.

It helped, but only a little. Parts of them were replaced by memories of helping her mother. A warm smile, a gentle hand, the taste popping in her mouth.

But underneath it all it was still there. Haunting, clutching. Forever to be entombed by nothing.

She shivered.

"What's cooking?" Zeld asked, slipping through the doorway.

"Beef stew. Or close enough," Stella said, glad of the interruption. She finished chopping the onions and slipped them in, along with the greens and potatoes.

"Smells good." Zeld took a seat at the dinner table, scrolling through something on her tablet. "What's the occasion?"

Stella wiped off her hands. "I didn't have one. Just thought people would like it." The cooker boiled and bubbled, sending steam up in plumes that spread throughout the combined cooking and dining chamber.

"Missing home?"

"Every day." Stella gave a half smile. "How about you?"

"Well, less when we keep having these issues with the scanners." Zeld screwed up her eyebrows and flicked onto another screen. "I keep telling Dave they need an overhaul. You know what he says."

"We can make do?" Stella said, hazarding a guess. Zeld gave her a look.

"If he puts it off one more year, I'm not sure I'm going to stick around."

"I wouldn't blame you." Stella turned to hide her discomfort, pretending to check on the stew. The cooker gave off waves of heat, so she turned it down to simmer.

"You seem off. Is everything okay?"

It came back. She squeezed her eyes shut, praying that the image would go away. The feeling, the touch. "Just homesick, like you said."

"You want to talk about it?" Stella turned. Zeld had set down her tablet and was staring intently at her.

"Not particularly."

"When you do, I'll be here."

"Thanks." Stella forced a smile, hoping that she wouldn't be found out. Zeld returned it, but her eyes lingered a little too long.

I've got to keep myself together, Stella thought. She busied herself with biscuits, mixing a batch of dough and trading small talk with Zeld, listening to her complain about the sensors.

She didn't catch most of it, but smiled and made polite noises in the right spots. The dough was tipped out onto the counter and she kneaded it. It was soft and cool, giving way beneath her hands.

Stella's heart churned, and her stomach tumbled. She clutched the edge of her bed with tight fists, willing the ship to stay back, stay away.

To just go on past and never encounter anything else like that again.

"Please assemble on the bridge," the ship said.

It was too late.

She willed herself to go, standing, then putting one foot in front of the other until she was there.

Everyone else was in the bridge. They didn't even turn to look at her when she entered.

"I'm not picking up anything," Zeld said at the console for the ship's auxiliary systems, including the sensors. She banged a hand on the side of it. "I told you we needed to fix the long-range sensors. They aren't giving us a good reading."

"What's wrong with them?" Dave asked.

"Something, I don't know what. I'm not a technician. I keep getting artefacts or... something else. False positives."

Dave frowned, then joined her. "Could it be a fake signal, from pirates?"

"Checking now." Zeld manipulated the console, working through different displays at an alarming rate. "Doesn't look like it. Short-range scanners are working fine and don't show anything out of the unusual."

"Alright, everyone to their stations. It looks like we'll have a search on our hands. We'll take it sector by sector, clearing anything in our path we think is most likely first." They all settled in for a long search.

At first the long-range scanner, although glitching, seemed to work. But as they spent more and more time in the area, it got worse.

Stella was distracted by space. Just a few inches between it and them, like a thin membrane. She didn't know why it bothered her now, but she kept imagining it rupturing, sucking the air and them out into the cold of space to freeze to death.

Of what she had heard it was a bad way to go. So cold it burned, then froze everything in your body. All the way down to your heart.

So she withdrew from the activity and conversation around her, staring into the black void of space.

Troubled by her memories and by what was to come.

"We'll move on. Looks like this sector's empty." Dave got up and stretched, then punched in the new coordinates. The ship responded, thrusters firing with a gentle acceleration that brought them in line. "Everyone, take a break. We'll be there in a few hours."

Stars streaked by, but Stella sat and watched. Dave waited, sitting with her and staring out.

"Anything you want to talk about?" He broke the silence first. The others had gone back to eat. The smell of rice and vegetables drifted into the control room.

"No." She shifted in the soft chair, worn by years of use.

Dave lingered, then left her.

The rest of the search was uneventful and took a few days. Stella walked through it like it was a dream state, wishing she were anywhere else.

A few days later, Zeld was at the scanner controls. "I've got some-thing." Everyone was around her in an instant.

The screen was fuzzy, but she pointed to a glowing blip in the haze, barely visible if you squinted. "It's worth checking out."

"Take us there." Dave stood over her shoulder, staring at it. Sally entered the course, and the ship turned.

"Wait, what was that?" A wave crossed over the screen, obscuring it. Zeld leaned in, changing the parameters. It lightened, darkened, but the blip didn't come back. "What do you think?" Dave asked.

"I think we need better long-range scanners," Zeld said, more than a touch of anger in her voice. "I don't know what's out there. It could be the ship, it was about the same signature."

"Zeld, how long until we get within short range scanning range?" Dave asked.

"Twenty minutes."

"Worth a shot," Sal said.

"Keep an eye out while we move." Dave rubbed his face. There were dark bags under his eyes. They all were feeling the stress.

Zeld turned, a frown on her face. She started to open her mouth.

"I don't want to hear it right now," Dave said, holding up a finger. His legs were spread and arms crossed.

Zeld shut her lips tightly and lowered her eyebrows, but didn't say anything else.

Stella stared out the window. Something drifted by, a bit of space junk, a small meteorite—she couldn't tell. She didn't feel much, wondered if this would be her last ship ride of her life.

What would life be like on Osuer? Growing up on a space station hadn't prepared her for life on a moon, let alone a planet.

"Almost there." Zeld was transfixed by her console, flashing and scrolling through all the displays so fast it would have given Stella a headache.

What was it like, at the final moments? She shivered to think of it.

"In range, taking the first scans now." The computer beeped and something flashed up on her console. "It's refining the return now."

The image on the screen, fuzzy and distorted, started to clear. It only took a few seconds to recognize the *Independence*.

Or what was left of her.

Andy let out a low whistle. "Cracked like an egg." It was a perfect explanation, the two halves drifting on the console and through space without power.

Dave sat in the pilot's chair, punched in the new coordinates, and the ship turned. "Fifteen minutes. Everyone gear up."

Stella bit her knuckle. The pain of it shot up her arm, but she didn't care. Instead, she bit harder, until it was so bad she almost cried.

"Stella?" Zeld was looking at her, an odd expression in her eyes.

She let go. "I'm going." She followed the others out into the equipment room. They were already putting their suits on, and she followed suit.

Stella had to keep telling herself it was the last time. The suit was cool, rough against her skin, and it squeezed tight. Less bulky than what they had back home, but still enough to restrict her movement, it was tough to maneuver inside.

It was the helmet that she dreaded. The tightness, the suffocation, the feeling of being enclosed. Once familiar, it was oppressive to think of.

Stella held her breath as she put it on, closing her eyes as it locked shut. That was enough. It was over now, and she took a deep breath of the recirculated air, so unique it was impossible to describe.

"Comms check," Dave said, a voice in her ear. She looked over to the floating display, triggering her ability to talk.

"Stella here." The others responded too, all working properly, if garbled by the age of the suits. Another of those things Dave never seemed to get around to fixing.

"Five minutes." The ship would be visible now, and the others crowded to the small window of the airlock.

"It's messed up. Whatever did that took no prisoners," Andy said, helmet pressed up against the glass. He let the others get in for their turn, but Stella kept far away. Let the others gawk.

"Time to walk," Dave said. They clustered into the airlock and shut the hatch behind them. The ship warned them of decompression, and they did the final suit check. The air was sucked out with a hiss.

"Decompression complete," the ship said.

"We don't have a good place to dock. You'll have to tether here and walk," Dave said. Stella wasn't sure if this was worse or better. In a few minutes there would be nothing but space between her and her suit.

When the doors flushed open they moved as one, Andy clipping on to the anchor point outside.

It was cold, despite the suit's warmers. Stars twinkled and glittered like glass, the glow of the Milky Way fuzzy like smoke around them. It took her breath away for a moment, all her fear and trepidation lost for a single, solitary moment.

"Stella?" Sally said. It broke the illusion.

"Coming." She grabbed her pack, slinging it on and clipping onto the line. Andy was out in front, a quick thruster fire, and flying toward the looming ship.

It trailed debris, frozen in space in the one horrific moment that it experienced. It took her breath away, but now the fear came back. What would be inside? What had happened to the crew?

The others were out pacing her, and she shook out of it to catch up, thrusting.

"Cargo hold will be on that side," Andy said, pointing to the larger section. "That's where the goods will be."

"If they survived," Dave added. "Remember, keep safe out there. That's your number one priority."

Stella wanted to be back on the ship, waiting for her chance to get off. Inside the familiar, cold ship that she had grown afraid of and was starting to hate. It had brought her out here.

"Coming left." Andy fired, turning into the bigger section. "I saw a door down there."

As soon as he said it her perspective shifted. The ship, once in front of her, now appeared to be beneath her, anchoring her in the vast darkness that surrounded them.

They were falling to it, dangling by a thin piece of metal, and the *Black Beauty* was far above.

Andy was the first to touch the *Independence*, the sound of him hitting the metal hull silent. All Stella could hear was the sound of her own breathing and the slight hum of the suit's electronics. All she could feel was the warmers against her skin and the hot breath blowing back in her face.

"We have touchdown." They all followed, Zeld, Sally, Sal, and finally Stella. Four out here, and one in the ship.

"Power's off. You'll have to cut your way through," Dave said.

"Hold on, I read about a mechanical override." Zeld reached around the door, gloved fingers searching and prying. "Here it is. Andy, give me a hand."

Together, grunting and puffing, they forced the hidden latch over, and the hatch shifted. Something like tiny shards of glass puffed out. Small crystals of water, freezing instantly in the infernal cold.

"Still pressurized." There was some level of awe in Zeld's voice.

"We could have survivors then."

"With no power?" Andy asked.

"We're not picking up any heat signatures here, but the hull is thick. They could have jumped in emergency stasis," Dave said.

"Or they could be dead," Sal said.

"Sal, keep on track. Get in there and get out." Dave sounded annoyed, but it didn't stop a chill from running down Stella's neck.

"Going in now." Andy pushed the hatch open the rest of the way. He activated his boots and clicked down onto the metal deck. The others followed, Stella in the rear. Her boots clanged on the deck, shaking her through her heels.

Their lights lanced into the dark ship, a dull glow from emergency lights near their feet keeping it from total darkness but not staving it off entirely. It was quiet.

No hum of machinery, no voices. Just... emptiness, like the space outside.

They walked deeper into the corridor, until it split into two. "I'll take one group left. Everyone else go with Zeld to the right." Andy divided them, taking Stella and Sally. They were here to salvage, not anything else, she kept telling herself.

"We should be able to get to the cargo hold this way," Andy said, opening a separate channel for their group only. Zeld had done the same, so that they wouldn't interfere with each other. Dave would be listening in on both of them on the *Beauty*. "Come on."

Stella didn't want to go into the dark corridor, afraid of what might be behind the next door or the next corner. She was starting to sweat, despite the coolness of space around her.

Things were suspended in the air, bits of broken hull, fragments of the ship, tools and things that had broken free in the accident.

Her mind wandered back to that as they clicked down the hallway. What had happened here?

Were they attacked? Hit by a stray meteorite?

Or was it sabotage, an explosion on the ship? But all of that was too dramatic. It was more likely they forgot to do some critical maintenance and something malfunctioned, exploding and killing everyone.

There were so many things on a ship that could kill you; it was like living on a bomb.

A flash of light illuminated something strange on the wall, and Stella was instantly drawn to it. She swept her own back over it.

Dark brown, but in a familiar shape. She couldn't put her finger on it at first.

And then, she remembered.

Brown, soft, and comforting. She almost smelled the mustiness of that old bear even now.

"What is it?" Sally asked.

Stella lingered, drawn to it. "Something from the past, an old teddy bear I had as a kid."

"Come on, you two." Andy was looking at his arm display, a floating projection of their best guess at the ship's interior hovering a few inches above it.

They were a white dot on the map, slightly flashing, with a route traced out.

"Checking in. How is everything?" Dave's voice crackled in her ear.

"Almost there, a few more turns," Andy said. "Otherwise, we're good."

Stella was starting to relax. They were good. Relatively unimpeded, the trip had gone smoothly. And, best part, there were no dead bodies.

No hands clutching at loved ones. No dead babies in their mother's arms.

The thought of it brought her to her knees, a wave of sickness washing over her.

"Stella, what's wrong?" Sally was at her side in a flash, shining a light into her helmet.

It was too bright, overwhelming, and Stella put up her hand to block it. "I'm okay," she whispered. "Just a little light-headed for a moment, that's all."

"Tell me if you need out of there." Dave's voice had a barely imperceptible layer of concern, too much for him normally. "I'll swap out with you."

"No, I can keep going." She got back to her feet, forcing the thoughts out of her. "I'm fine now." She breathed the recirculated air, closing her eyes for a moment.

"Have you found... anyone?" Dave asked.

"No, not a thing," Andy said, eyebrows creased in concern as he studied her. She gave him a smile, which was enough to satisfy him. He turned back to the map, leading them the last few turns to the cargo hold.

"Jackpot," Andy said. The door was up ahead, larger than the side passages and rooms. This one was big enough to admit a hovercart, or two. He went up to the controls. "Locked. Or might as well should be." He tried touching it, the panel giving a decidedly loud warning at his touch.

"We're going to need power restored," Andy said, keying to the other group's channel. "Any luck so far?"

"We're at the emergency power room now," Zeld said. "Boy, it's a mess."

"Should we crack it then?" Andy asked.

"Give her a few minutes to work her magic," Dave said. "With any luck you won't have to."

"Got it. Guess we'll sit tight." Andy started wandering down the hallway.

"What are you doing?" Sally asked. "You said we'd sit tight."

"Just looking around. No harm in that, is there?" Stella sat down on her kit. She didn't want to explore at all.

"We should at least stick together."

"Why? You can wait here."

"You can't mean that. This place gives me the creeps, you can't feel it?"

Andy shrugged. "Just a piece of salvage. Space junk floating into the great unknown. Nothing to fear about that."

"You aren't leaving us alone."

"Come on then." Andy waved for them to come with him. "We won't go far. Besides, there might be something worth looking for."

"They must have been in the front half of the ship," Stella said softly.

"What?" The others turned to her.

"The crew. They must have been in the front half of the ship when it... broke."

Andy paused. "Makes sense. Anyway, are you guys coming?" He didn't wait, but turned down the corridor from where they came.

Sally pulled Stella up. "Come on, I'm not going alone."

They followed Andy, walking back down to the first door they saw. It was also locked, so they tried another. Same result.

"Can't even get into the side compartments." Andy tapped on the front of his helmet. It made a small tunk that fed into his communicator. "If they don't get this ship up and running soon, we'll have to pry them open."

"Or cut them," Sally suggested. "It'll be quicker."

"Won't that leave an obvious trace we were here?" Andy asked.

"And prying them open wouldn't?"

"Good point. Dave, any ETA on normal power."

"Negative. Proceed with destructive entry as needed." Andy grinned.

"You heard the man, let's get to work." A short trip back to the tools later, Stella set off the cutting torch, refining the plasma flare down to a fine point.

She moved it to the point she thought would make the most impact, near the center of the door. It had a larger bulge, and she guessed it was the locking mechanism.

Like a surgeon she sliced right at the door seal, barely a burn on the door itself. She turned off her plasma torch. "Try it now."

Andy and Sally grabbed a hold and pulled it back. It ground on the track, but slowly opened with enough force.

"Good work," Andy said, examining her quick and efficient handiwork. The lock was sliced clean, the ripple of the plasma torch visible on the metal.

"Thanks." She smiled a true smile. It felt good to be useful again, after so long in space doing nothing.

This was what she thought Dave would miss the most. No one else on the team had the same skill with a plasma torch. For general salvage it didn't matter as much, but what they did made it critical.

"Should we cut open the cargo hold?" Stella asked. "I think I know where to cut."

"Negative, for now. I've put the others on a clock. If they can't get the ship up and running again, I'll set you on it."

It made sense, there was only so much fuel on board the ship, and they'd already used some of it. A door like that was going to take most of what they had, if not all of it.

After she packed up her equipment Stella pulled out the small, hand held cutter. The fuel gage was full, and it wouldn't cut through much, but fit in her pocket nicely. She slipped it inside, patting it, and closed the case.

Andy and Sally were at the door. Their lights lanced into the room. It used to be a bedroom, but didn't look like anyone had lived in it a while.

There was a bed, still made, an empty desk, and little else in the room.

"Weird," Sally said, following Andy inside. Stella put up her equipment, stowing back inside the case and locking it tight.

Something moving out of the corner of her eye caught her attention, deeper into the ship. Before she could swing her light toward it, it was gone.

The hairs on the back of her neck stood up. "Did you see that?" she asked.

"See what?" Lights swung toward her, and she stared at the spot. There was nothing.

"Nothing. Just my imagination." The darkness was complete down that way, not even the emergency lighting was on. Stella took a few calming breaths, closed her eyes for a second, then shot open when she imagined something coming up to her.

There was nothing there. Still.

She latched her case and backed up into the room. The corridor was quiet, and completely still.

"Not much here. I'm thinking it was an empty room." Andy shuffled through the drawers on the desk, all empty.

"Why would they leave it empty?"

"Beats me. I guess they were down on manning and had a spare. Or used to carry travelers for a little bit of extra cash."

Sally opened the wardrobe, a few scraps of cloth crumpled up in the bottom. She leaned down and turned them over.

"I don't understand why. Why not use the space if you have it, all they were shipping was protein."

"Don't ask me. I'm not in charge." Andy finished at the desk, then came back out. "What do you think, go for another one?"

Stella shrugged. "We've got enough for a few more, unless we have to cut through that hatch."

"Best not risk it then. I'll pry one open." He moved down the corridor and started in on the door, forcing his prying tool into the small space.

It didn't go well, the tool was too big, but he kept at it, opening up the metal hit by hit. Soon he was huffing and puffing, with little to show for it.

"Anyone else want to try?" He held up his pry bar.

"No thanks." Sally made a face at him. Stella shook her head. She couldn't get that odd sensation out of her head.

"Beauty, come in. Any ETA on that power?"

"Zeld thinks they have a solution, rerouting a few links by hand. Give them another ten minutes."

"You heard the man, just enough time to break in." He went back to work, slamming and grinding against the metal. The sound echoed in the silent ship.

Eventually, he made a hole big enough for his pry bar to get through. With one last pull he snapped something inside, and the door popped open.

"Well look at this." His light shone inside. Stella and Sally joined him, looking over his shoulder. "Military grade stuff."

The room had been converted to an armory, filled with rifles and pistols of every sort.

"What kind of transport needs weapons this far into space?" Sally asked. Andy walked inside and picked up a rifle.

"Expensive too. This has the latest laser compression tech. Whoever bought this spared no expense." He raised it to his shoulder and sighted down.

"There weren't any arms listed, were there?"

Stella asked.

"Not that I saw. Dave, you catching this?"

"I see it."

"What do you think?" Andy asked.

"I'm not sure I like this job anymore. I'm checking with my sources now. There's also chatter in the airwaves. We're not the only ones looking for this ship, and whoever else is out there is keeping quiet with shortwave comms."

"We should leave," Stella said, that oppressive feeling coming back even stronger.

"They're almost done with the power, two minutes tops. Might as well take a look since you're down there," Dave said.

"We'll go back to the cargo bay now," Andy said. "In the mean time, might as well take a few of these." He strapped a few pistols on, tossing one to Sally and offering another to Stella. She shook her head, and he shrugged.

He took a few more rifles, slinging them over his shoulder, and they went back to the cargo hold hatch. Just as they were turning the corner the lights flickered, then turned on.

"Let there be light," Andy said, switching off his light. Stella took a quick look around. They were alone.

The ship hummed to life, vibrating through the floors. "Power's on now. We'll see if we can get that door open," Sally said. Gravity pulled them to the floor, restored with the power.

Stella dropped her case, letting Sally and Andy take the lead on the door while she looked around. It was standard construction, solid but nothing fancy, with metal paneling along the corridor to cover the services and power lines that ran throughout the ship.

The floors were clean, if a little dusty, and showed their footprints very faintly. She leaned down, her eye catching something odd in the dust.

It was some form she had never seen. Not unlike an animal track, or what she had read and seen of them, it had three prongs.

"Got it," Andy said, pumping a fist in the air as the hatch started to unlock. The pins drew back, then the door pulled in and swung into the cargo hold.

An empty cargo hold, except one case in the center of the room strapped down.

"Dave, we got a problem," Andy said. "Where is all the cargo?"

Stella thought she saw something move again, just out of the periphery of her vision, but, once again, it was gone before she could get a good look.

"I think we should leave," she said, softly.

"This doesn't make sense," Dave said, a hint of concern in his voice.

"The intel I had on this was good."

"It doesn't matter," Andy said, moving into the cargo hold. "Whatever you got was wrong. Or someone's been here ahead of us."

"No one's been here," Stella said. "It was locked too tightly. And why would they leave this if they took everything else?"

"Hold tight. I'm sending everyone else your way," Dave said.

"They'll be there in about ten minutes."

"What a complete bust," Andy said. The glow of light in the cargo hold was dimmer than the corridors, a few of the lights were broken. Stella took a closer look at them. They weren't intact anymore. Something had happened to them.

"Look at those," Sally said, pointing to the lights. "Are they..."

"I think so too." Stella felt something rise up in her belly. She turned to look in the corridor. It was still empty, but that feeling didn't go away. The helmet was hot and stuffy, almost oppressive.

"Why would there be burn marks on the ceiling?" Andy asked. They were a few inches deep in spots, sometimes less. Either way, deep black scars went through the ceiling and the lights like a criss-cross pattern.

"Can we leave?" Stella asked, an ache starting at the back of her head. "I think we should get out of here."

"Hold on, I want to see what's up there." Andy started into the room, his footsteps lost in the cavernous feeling of it.

"Wait," Stella said, but Sally was following close behind. Andy had weapons training and had most of the guns. Stella rushed after them.

"Come on, we'll stick together."

"What are those markings on the side?" Sally asked. They were strange, something Stella had never seen before.

"Running it through the database now. No initial hits, it may have to go off hull." Dave had regained his calm tone. "Other team is about five minutes out."

They were at the object now, big, metal. The top was open, whatever used to be the lid peeking out from behind it. When they got close enough, it was obvious to see why.

"Something isn't right." Stella held back from the other two.

Andy walked around, leaned down to examine the strange marks on it. "Whatever happened to it wasn't good. Look at these, they're deep. And it's at least two inches thick."

He traced the marks that ran down like gashes, bits of metal pushed off to the side like butter.

"You sure they were transporting proteins?" Andy asked Dave.

"Not anymore. Still haven't found out what that symbol is, but I'm coming in to evacuate you. Pick up the other team and come to the hatch you came from. I'm switching channels now."

"Almost there," Zeld said, a few more contacts popping up in Stella's display. What did you guys do to this door?"

"Cut it open," Andy said. He was climbing up on the box now. He let out a loud whistle, then cursed. "What is this thing?"

Stella didn't want to see it, didn't care about it anymore. She wanted to get out. "We can meet them at the door, come on." She tugged on Sally's arm, pulling her to the door.

"Can you let us in? We had to come up the other side," Zeld said. Stella looked at the distance to the other door, and the wide open space in between. She didn't want to go there.

"Why did you take that way?" she asked, not able to stop the irritation from showing in her voice.

"It was faster than going around, by about half. Let us in, will you?"

"Come on," Andy said, starting forward. "You've missed quite a lot since you restored power."

"And I think you might have activated some sort of beacon. I'm getting transmissions from the ship," Dave said. They were at the door now, and Andy was fiddling around with it, trying to get it open. Stella clutched herself, looking around. There was an eerie feeling around her.

She couldn't quite place it, but the lack of light didn't help any. She kept jumping at shapes that turned out to be their shadows when she had more time to look at them.

"Hurry up. We need to get out."

"Can't figure out how to get it open."

"You have to unlock it," Zeld said.

"Thank you so much for the help," Andy said, his voice dripping with sarcasm. "Give me a few more minutes."

The lights in the corridor flickered. Stella looked hard, focusing her attention on it and holding her breath.

Her heart was pounding in her chest, oppressive and pinched. The suit was restrictive, almost too much. She longed to be off, to be out of it, to be anywhere but here.

This was nothing compared to the bodies. The images still came back to her.

Women clutching their own babies, frozen in space. Children curled up into balls. The bile rose in her mouth and she tried to hold it down.

"We need to leave." Stella shrank back from the door they had come from as the light flickered again.

"I'm picking up some unusual activity," Dave said. "I'm coming in close. You need to be at the airlock in three minutes."

"Hurry up with that door," Sally said.

"I'm going," Andy said, hunched over the controls. His hands worked furiously.

"Too late," Stella said. It was there, in the corridor.

"Got it!" The hatch slid open, revealing the others. Stella stepped back, then took another. "Good to see you all."

They conversed behind her, unaware of the danger ahead.

"Go back, shut the door!" Stella turned and pushed them out. "Shut it now!"

"What's going on down there?" Dave said. Confusion rang as everyone started talking at once, then Sally screamed.

The figure was moving into the cargo bay.

Andy let out a long stream of curses. "What is that?"

Stella's hands shook, and the blood rushed in her ears. She gasped for breath, her throat constricted. In a second she was at the controls. "Get in here." She pulled at the nearest body, she didn't know who it was.

Sharp clicks. Andy was firing. Light flashed with every shot, but it didn't seem to do anything. Hisses, as the air started leaking from the ship.

It was pure confusion, but the crew was mostly out of the cargo bay. Stella worked the controls, found where to shut it, and did. "Andy, get in here."

The door was moving, sliding into position to shut. Andy was still on the other side, firing away. "Get back, you piece of shit. Get back!"

He turned to run, his face desperate. He only had a few steps to go, but the figure moved fast.

It was on him before he could make it, pulling him back into the cargo bay. Stella caught a momentary glimpse of sharp teeth or claws.

Then she was sprayed with something. She flinched, recoiling. Andy screamed, his voice cut off in a gurgle a second later.

A second later the doors shut. Sickening, crunching noises came through the comms, then they went dark.

Stella blinked, wiping the blood off her helmet. Beside her Sally was sick in her own helmet. Her ears were ringing, the world suddenly going numb.

She held up her hand, stained red.

People were panicking, talking over each other on the comms channel.

Finally, Dave broke through the chatter. "Everyone shut up." They went quiet, one by one. This wasn't supposed to happen. She didn't sign up for this. "Listen, if you want to get out of there, I need you to get outside the ship." His voice was shaking. "I can swing around to that side."

Stella reached out for Sally, touching her back. She was sobbing.

"There's an airlock on this side, closer to the engine room. We passed it on the way," Zeld said, staring at the door, blanched.

"What about Andy? We can't leave him—"

"Andy's dead. Get your asses moving."

"What was that?" Sal asked. They were all thinking the same thing. Stella hadn't got a good look at it, but what she saw was more than enough to satisfy her curiosity.

"Focus. Get out of that ship. I'm bringing the *Beauty* around now," Dave said.

Zeld got up, then pulled Sal to his feet. Her breathing was hard between words. "This way."

Stella didn't want to stay there, but she didn't want to move either. "This ship wasn't transporting proteins, was it?"

"It doesn't matter," Zeld said, starting down the corridor. That thing in there had been the cargo, a type of protein.

And it hadn't been too friendly.

Stella pulled Sally to her feet. "Come on." Her vomit stained the helmet, but there wasn't anything Stella could do. She went willingly, like a doll that needed someone to move it.

It must smell horrible in there. There was no way to clean it now, not like this. Even if they had the time. So all Stella could do was support her, and rub her back to make her feel better as they walked down the hallway.

It looked similar to the other side. All metal ribs and lights.

Something caught her eye. All along the wall there were dark stains.

A brief memory of the other corridor came back to her. She thought they were just strange designs, a foreign type of art. Now, she knew better.

It was blood.

Her stomach recoiled, her previous meal rising in her throat. **She** fought it down. There was no way to get it out, but then the wave of nausea passed and lessened, still there but far at the back of her mind.

They had to get out of here. The corridor stretched off in the distance, an impossible way. Behind her, farther back in the direction they had come, there was pounding running through the ship.

"The ship is depressurizing," Zeld said in between breaths. There was a pop and crunch. "That's all."

Or was it that... thing coming through the door three inches thick? Now, all the signs made sense. They were there the whole time, from the guns to the reinforcement in the box.

But whatever precautions they had taken failed.

The pit in her stomach was bigger now, threatening to swallow up her courage. There was little help left for them.

The lights flickered.

"What was that?" Sally asked, a hint of panic in her voice. She was breathing heavily, along with the others, between where the mic cut out.

"Not sure. We stabilized the generator and had it up and running right," Zeld said. She searched both sides of the corridor. "There was plenty of fuel left, so it can't be running out."

"You all need to get to the hatch as soon as you can," Dave said. "I'm almost in position now."

"Give us five minutes," Sal said. The sides of the ship seemed to compress, pushing against her. Stella wished they could be off now. Why did they have to wait?

Less than a minute later the lights flickered again, then went dead. Stella jerked back, scrambling in the dark to turn on her light. Her body floated, released by the artificial gravity that was now gone.

The others were doing the same thing, and lights flashed on, cutting through the complete darkness. Everyone was talking at once, asking questions.

It was overwhelming. Sally sat down and clutched at her helmet. Stella wanted to go back.

Only Zeld was calm. "Dave, we've got another power failure, and the backup isn't coming on either."

"I know."

"What aren't you telling us?" she asked. "Quiet, everyone." She cut through the chatter and they went still. Somehow the silence was even more oppressive.

Stella took a few deep breaths of the recirculated air in her helmet, thick with sweat. It had been hours since she put it on, but with the loss of gravity with the power, the weight was gone.

"Whatever was in the cargo bay is moving," Dave said after a long pause. He was conflicted, she could hear it in his voice. "The best thing you can do is get to that hatch. Please."

That spurred them to action, all lights swiveling to the corridor. They had to magnetize their boots and move, which slowed them down. Each foot took extra concentration, requiring a brief second before they could lift the other. Her heart was beating fast, and every second she expected to see something in the lights.

Stella's hand found the pistol Andy had given her. What was she going to do with it? She was a field tech, not a fighter.

"Just up ahead," Sal said, "around that corner."

Her hands were shaking now, from the fear that tried to devour her. But that thing could be behind them too. The thought struck at her, lancing into her mind.

She didn't turn around. If she kept looking ahead, then there wouldn't be anything back there. The thought was foolish, but she let herself be convinced.

"There it is," Zeld said. Her light fixed on an opening in the corridor, on the hull side. "Everyone get out as fast as you can."

"It's not working." Sal was at the door first, hopelessly trying to manipulate the dead controls. "We can't get out without the power back on."

"Let me see it," Stella said, pushing away her fear and approaching the door. The distraction helped as she examined the hatch.

Her light revealed a standard airlock entrance with four hinges, two on each side, and a sealed center portion. Beyond that, through the glass window, was the airlock itself, then the freedom of space. Stars glimmered through the outer airlock window.

She tried to push aside the seal, but it wouldn't move. There had to be some way to keep it shut, but how?

"Anyone have a scanner?" she asked.

"Here." Zeld handed it to her. Stella checked the top and bottom, then the seal itself. "Well?"

"It's got two bolts on the top and two on the bottom holding it in. With power we could retract them, but I don't have enough juice to get through them with this." Stella pulled out her mobile cutter. "Maybe one, two at most. That still leaves us the outer airlock door."

"Which means you can't do it," Sal said.

Stella shook her head. "No, I can't."

"We'll go back to the engine room and turn on the power then," Zeld said, stepping forward. "With a total failure like this, the core must have been turned off. I can get it back on if I work fast enough."

"What turned off the power to begin with?" Sally asked. No one said anything. "Dave?"

"I'm here."

"Did you hear my question?"

"I heard. I..."

"I'm not going back there with that thing. No way." Sally backed up.

"I don't think we have a choice, unless you want to stay here with it." Zeld crossed her arms, pursing her lips. "We can either die here not doing anything or die trying."

Stella didn't know what to think. Her head was swimming. They were trapped on this ship with whatever it was that killed the first crew and ate them. How long would it be until it found them?

Her stomach roiled and rebelled. There weren't enough hours in the day to do this, and enough money to keep her here. She regretted ever signing up for this job.

Stella shut her eyes, leaning her head back against the edge of her helmet. All she wanted was to see the galaxy, to explore and learn. And now, this.

"I don't want to go," Sally said, almost hysterical. "I have to get out of here."

"That's what we're all going to do." Zeld took hold of her shoulders, but Sally tried to push her off.

"Let go of me."

Zeld only tightened her grip. "Sally, you need to calm down. I want you to relax. You're no good to us like this."

"Please don't make me go there," Sally said, trembling. She had stopped fighting, and Zeld pulled her into an embrace. "I don't want to." Her voice was cracked and high-pitched.

"We aren't going to get off this ship, are we?" Stella looked down at the pistol. She could end it here, before it got too bad. One shot was all it would take. Then, oblivion.

And then she would never see her family again. Her mother, her father. Never again.

"I'll get you out of there. I'm coming out to open the hatch," Dave said. His voice was muffled; he was getting into a suit. "*Beauty* can take care of herself for now, but I'm taking the cutter over there and doing it myself. Stella, open up that door like a can of beans."

He was coming across, despite the storm that forced him off. Why would he do that?

She knew it was for the crew. He loved them like family, and they loved him back. It felt bitter that she would be leaving him, leaving what could have been.

It took a few seconds of hesitation, then a prompt by Zeld, for Stella to take out her portable cutter. She crouched down and turned it on, adjusting the flame to the minimum size she thought would cut through to conserve fuel. For a second she thought about her pack, far back behind them in the cargo bay, and wished she had taken it with her.

But there it was, and there it would remain. No way would she be going back into that room again. The thought of it made her skin crawl. The remains of Andy...

The torch touched the edge of the door as she got to work, sizzling through the seal before it hit the whine of metal. She moved it back and forth while the others looked on anxiously, gathered around her in a huddle.

It was oppressive, and she paused momentarily. "Will you give me some room?"

They apologized and backed up, glancing back down the corridor from where they had come. She felt it **too**, that need to go as fast as possible, that desire to get out of here, but she held back as much as she could.

She needed to get this right.

Already the fuel gauge was emptying, about a quarter gone. The sound changed, and the feel, and she thought she was through one.

Now she turned her attention to the top. It was higher than she could reach. "Anyone see anything that could get me up there?"

"No, I haven't seen anything." The others looked around, peering around the corner cautiously. Again, her case would have gotten her there. As it was, she only needed to get up a foot and a half or so to be comfortable.

"I'll check the other rooms," Sal said, starting back where they had come from.

"That's no use. They're all locked without power, and I don't have the fuel or time to get them open." She frowned, staring at the door.

A clunk on the hull startled her, but then Dave's helmeted face entered the window of the exterior hatch. "I'm on. Give me a few and I'll get you out." The sounds of him preparing came through the hull, but didn't help them any.

"Give me a boost," Stella said. "You'll have to help me."

"Are you sure?" Zeld asked.

"As long as you hold me down, I won't float away."

She kicked off her magnets, floating up to the second set of bolts at the top. This was going to be interesting, and the angle she was at wasn't helping. Stella tried balancing on her feet, leaning over while she was attached to the door itself, but couldn't get into position.

"I need some help here. Will someone hold me down?" She floated back into space, giving them something to grab onto in the form of her legs.

"Got you," Sal said, grabbing one leg while Zeld took the other. She directed them until she could get into position and set about cutting.

It was more difficult, at a strange angle. She had her arms outstretched, her wrist bent over, to reach. It wasn't the best position, but she didn't have a choice.

Something was on this ship, and she didn't want to be here any longer. So, instead of spending the time to get a better position, she cut.

The cutter burned through the metal, sparks flashing every so often and illuminating the others with a garish light. Stella cut, sweeping through the bolt at the top.

She had her wish, she thought as she worked. This wasn't a ship filled with dead refugees. She didn't need to wade through their floating bodies to get to the cargo.

No, this was a much better blessing, she thought with a grim face. This was much better.

Dave worked the other side, cutting through the exterior. He had a mechanical saw, and it ground against the metal with a horrible sound.

Finally, the bolt gave way, and her cutter slid through. "Got it. Bring me down."

"Get it open," Zeld said.

"We have to get out," Sally said, eyes wide with terror. They grabbed onto the seal and tried pulling it open.

The door shifted, but held. "Stand back," Stella said. She cut the door seal, giving them enough room to put their gloved hands in and also sever any tie that was too small to see with the scanner.

Then her cutter fluttered and died. It still registered a quarter tank of fuel, and she pounded it against the door in anger, cursing. "I'm out of fuel."

"Almost through the exterior hatch," Dave said. Stella tried to turn it on again. Nothing. She shook it, hoping to free something, and tried again.

This time it worked. She tried to finish the seal, but it was sputtering.

"We need to leave." Sally backed up into her.

"Watch out," Stella said angrily. The bump had thrown her off, cutting a chunk out of the door itself, and the cutter was dead once again.

"Run," Sal said. Stella whipped her head around, and her light caught the black, smooth skin of something crawling on the ceiling.

Her heart, already beating fast, kicked into overdrive. The thing was less than a few yards away. She turned and ran with the others, hampered by the weightlessness. Behind her something clicked on the ceiling.

Breathing hard and fast, they fled into the ship. Sal was in the lead, and Dave was shouting at them over the comms, urging them to come back.

Then, he stopped. "What was that?" he asked.

No one bothered to stop to tell him. Hard breathing as they ran was all that went across the comms.

Then Sally cried out. Stella turned to look back. She was kneeling, trying to get up. Her vomit-stained helmet couldn't hide the plea for help in her eyes. She stretched out an arm to Stella.

Stella stopped and started to turn, but then the thing descended onto Sally.

It was gone, and Sally's hand floated toward her. That was all that was left of her.

Sheer terror took her. Stella ran, overcome. Thoughts fled her, and time seemed to slow.

Zeld was ahead of her, screaming at her, motioning her into a side door.

Time slowed.

The weightlessness dragged at her.

Held her back.

But she ignored it, the fire of fear flowing through her.

A few more steps.

Then hands on her arms pulling.

And she was through.

Sal and Zeld struggled with the door, pushing it shut. Stella threw her weight into the door. They had to get it shut before that thing came through.

The door shut with a clang, and Sal pulled on the mechanical lock. Somehow it worked.

Gasping, Stella backed away from the door and hit something behind her. She spun, but it was just a wall.

"What is this place?" she asked. It was a small hallway, with a low ceiling. Her lungs were burning and her heart throbbed with terror still.

"A maintenance corridor," Sal said, then pushed past her. "Come on, this way." He sounded calm somehow, if a bit breathless. "I saw it on the maps and hoped it would be open."

"Wait, you're just going to leave her?" Stella asked as Zeld followed.

"She's dead, Stella. There's no one to leave." Zeld's voice was cold, but shaking. "If you want to stay here, then be my guest."

"Is everyone okay?" Dave asked.

"No, everyone isn't okay, Dave," Stella said, her frayed nerves making her snap at him. Anger bubbled up, and she clutched at it to drive away some of her fear. Still, she followed the others. "Sally is... she's... gone."

The look in her eyes. That form descending on her. Stella shuddered, almost overcome with fear again. She wanted to stop, to hide, to get out of here.

She wanted to scream.

"If you can get back here—"

"Not in a million years," Sal said, shaking his head. "Not with that thing in the way." They came to a crossroads in the corridor. "Left."

"Where are you taking us?" Zeld asked.

"Back to where we came in. We can slip out while that thing is on this side of the ship." Sal swallowed. "I hope."

"We aren't going to get out of here alive." Hopelessness swallowed up Stella's anger. She wanted to sit down, she wanted to cry.

Zeld rounded on her. "That's enough of that," she snapped. "I don't want to hear it."

"Everyone stay calm," Dave said. "I'm going back to the ship, and I'll provide overwatch." The corridor was eerie without lights. It felt like a tomb, and they were unwelcome with their lancing lights.

Their footsteps clanking on the metal floor echoed, muffled by her helmet. Who was watching them while Dave was in space, headed back to the ship? Her heart was still pumping fast, and Stella wasn't sure she had calmed down yet.

But she didn't have time to dwell on it. They pulled her through the passage, through twists and turns that had her lost in no time. She could have been going back to the cargo room for all she knew.

"One more turn and we'll be there." Sal was hunched over, forced into that position by the height of the ceiling. She wanted to let go and fly through the hallway, and she kept looking back over her shoulder, thinking that thing would be there.

Each time, her light illuminated nothing but cold metal.

She checked her suit status. Over half a charge left, but less than a quarter of her oxygen remained, even with the recirculation capturing what she breathed out.

The others had to be at or near the same levels. "We need to hurry."

"Calm down, Stella," Zeld said. It was infuriating how calm she was. The older woman had been through a lot as a salvager, but had she been in situations like this?

"Almost back. Not sure what things are going to be like on the *Independence*." Dave was breathing heavily, but it was welcome to hear his voice.

She was going to miss him the most, out of all of them. The thought struck her, as silly as it seemed, in the middle of the run. Why, she wasn't sure. However, the effect his voice had on her was calming.

The tunnel was too small for that thing. They were safe here, and Dave was going to help them get out. She took a deep breath and tried to calm her nerves.

"Here it is." Sal stopped, a door up ahead. "We're on the other side of the ship." He flicked his wrist, and a map came up on her display.

It was the *Independence*, with a flashing blue dot showing where they were. She gulped. It was a bigger ship than she realized, if it took them all that time to get across it. "Here." Sal zoomed in, then traced a path to the escape hatch. It was the same one they had come in. "Just a few minutes and we'll make it."

Stella stared at the door. It could be on the other side for all they knew. How fast did it go?

"We should wait until Dave gets back to the ship," she said.

Zeld shook her head. "We don't have enough time. We should go now, while we still have the chance."

"I'm with you." Sal turned back to the door. "Help me with this."

They started opening it when Dave came back. "I'm almost in, decompressing now. Give me thirty seconds."

The others stopped, halfway into opening the door, and looked at each other. They turned to the door. "Maybe we can wait," Sal said.

Zeld backed up and leaned against the wall. Her face was serene and calm.

"How can you be so calm?" Stella asked, the words out of her mouth before she could even stop them. Her hand shook, and her legs felt like jelly.

Zeld shrugged. "I've been out here a long time. Seen a lot of things. I suppose getting all worked up would be fine for others, but I haven't seen the use."

"That's why she's on the team," Sal said, slipping down to sit. "Always calm under pressure, no matter what happens."

"I couldn't do it." Stella looked down at her hands, flecks of blood sprayed across her suit. Some of it was Sally's. She shivered, getting sick again and fighting it off. "I'm not going to do it, if we get out of here."

"When. When we get out of here." Zeld stared at her fiercely, eyes blazing. "I don't want to hear anything differently. Say it."

"When," she murmured.

"I know the last job didn't go well, and that you saw some things," Zeld said. "And I can't help that. Our job right now is to get off this ship and get the hell out of here." She reached across, put a hand on hers, calming the shaking. Stella looked up, back into her eyes. "No matter what you think will happen, we have to stay together. We're family."

The nausea calmed, and a wave of sadness replaced it. The lull made everything real now. Andy, Sally, they were dead and gone. No one but them would mourn them.

Her family.

She touched the wall, hard against her glove. The glove protected her from what must have been the cold. It would drain the heat from her in an instant.

Like whatever followed them would do to their life.

"We've been in worse situations," Zeld said, still staring at her. Stella wanted to curl into a ball and cry, but she couldn't do it in front of them.

"Like what?" She kept the trembling from her voice, but barely. Her arms wrapped around her body, her breath making little puffs against the plastic of her visor.

"Like when the Republic caught us salvaging their cruiser. I thought they were going to blow us out of space. If it wasn't for Dave's piloting, they would have. Isn't that right, Dave?"

There was nothing. "Dave?" Zeld stood up.

"I'm here. Having a bit of a problem with the decompression sequence."

Zeld growled. "Isn't that something I told you to have fixed in Europa?"

"*Beauty's* on it. Give me a few minutes. In the meantime, I'll see what I can do about your overwatch."

"He can't get a display in there," Sal said.

"No. But he might be able to patch in a feed. That means we either sit tight for the next five to ten minutes, or we risk it and try and get out on our own."

Neither option sounded appealing. Stella licked her dry lips. They were salty, and only served to remind her of her thirst. She took a drink of the tepid suit water, watching the level drop to near zero.

Now she was out of water too. She longed to be back home, or even back on the *Beauty*. She would be sitting around the table with the others, laughing and eating, having a good time. Fresh food, clear running water. It was a dream, but she felt comfort in it anyway.

Sal cleared his throat. "I say we go for it. The longer we wait, the less likely we have a chance to get out."

"No!" Stella swallowed, not sure why she had yelled out so much. "No, we should wait for Dave."

"Who says it hasn't gotten into the maintenance tunnels already?" Sal bore into her with an uncomfortable gaze. There was sweat on his brow, despite the cold. She wasn't the only one afraid.

"It's too big."

"You don't know that it can't get smaller, squeeze into that opening we left it."

"Sal," Zeld said, eyebrows knit together, her most motherly stare.

"He's right. We don't know anything. It could be in here." They all turned to the tunnel behind them. Stella took an unconscious step back to the door.

"Well, you're the deciding vote, Zeld. What's it going to be?" Sal turned to her, shining his light in her face.

Zeld looked down, concentrated. Stella wished she knew what she was thinking, considering. She felt the urge to flee, but realized that door might be the only thing in between it and them.

Visions flashed by, of the door being ripped off the hinges, that thing coming inside.

Devouring them all. Bite by bite. Chunk by chunk.

They would be nothing but splashes on the wall. Artwork that was meant for no one, too macabre for words.

"Let's go. We aren't going to get out of here waiting around." Zeld stood, puffs of her breath fogging a small section of her visor. "But if we're going to do this we need to do it fast. Unattached."

"If you just wait…" Dave said, breathing hard.

"We don't have the luxury," Sal said. "Unless you want to come down and switch places with it." Sal tapped on his wrist, then flung up the route to them. "Just a few yards to the right, then one turn, then we're home free."

Zeld grabbed Stella's shoulders and turned her to look in her eyes. She was probing, but the eyes were soft and steady. Behind them was the hardness of survival. "Stella, stay with me and we'll make it out of here. You're going to buy me a big cup of Chava when we get to Sirus."

Stella looked back, then nodded. "And Dave will finally fix the sensors." A smile turned up the corners of her mouth, and Zeld returned it.

"He'll owe us that, at the least."

"I won't owe you anything. If anything, you'll owe me," Dave said, crackling through.

"Everyone ready?" Zeld asked. They nodded. "We'll make a break for it. Here we go." There was only enough room for two of them to work the hatch, and Stella let Zeld and Sal take hold of it.

After some grunting and straining, they broke it free of whatever position it had locked itself into over the years. It squealed and squeaked. Sal cursed.

"That'll bring it right to us."

"Too late," Zeld said. "Keep going. We can make a run." Stella watched anxiously. If she had her hands free she would have resorted to chewing her fingernails like she had as a child.

After what seemed like ages the hatch ring stopped. Sal pushed his shoulder against it and shoved with all his might, Zeld standing behind and over him, aiding him.

The door opened into gaping darkness.

It stared at her, tried to swallow her up. Stella was transfixed.

It was shattered by Sal's light, then lanced by Zeld's.

"Go." Zeld kicked off the ground, right behind Sal. They floated into the hallway, then spun and pushed off the hatch to the right.

It slammed back. A flash of black reflected her light.

Stella screamed.

Sal tried to turn, but his head floated free of his body. Tiny droplets of his blood pooled from his neck, then drifted away as a gush of a bubble grew.

Stella scrambled back. Her ears rang and her head swam. She kicked free of the magnets and rocketed through the maintenance tunnels.

Left, right, it was all a blur to her. She was vaguely aware of voices in her ear, but she was too panicked to listen to them.

"Stella!" Dave was panicked too, but his voice was something she could grasp, something real.

"Dave?" Her voice was weak. She turned down another tunnel and crouched down, holding onto a pipe running along the wall.

There were sounds, Zeld breathing and straining. She couldn't get them out of her head.

"I'm here. Stella, what's going on?"

Floating bubbles of blood. Sal's head, gone. Stella couldn't handle it anymore. She broke down and cried.

Tears flowed out of her eyes, pooling up in bubbles that she couldn't get off. She blinked, but they just stuck to her eyelashes.

She was blubbering, but what else could she do? She was never going to make it out of here alive.

"Stella, calm down." It was Zeld's voice. She was still calm, despite the breathing.

"Zeld, what happened?" Dave asked.

"It got Sal."

Dave cursed. "I'm coming back down there."

"How is that going to help?" Zeld asked. Stella was still crying hot tears, trying to shake them away. They floated in her helmet. All of the emotions rushed out of her, and her legs shook.

Stella dropped to the ground, curling up. Everything she had ever known, it was all for nothing. She would have no family, no loved ones down here. This ship would be her grave.

"I got away," Zeld was saying. "It stopped to—" she choked up. "To feed."

"I'm in. *Beauty*, hook me up." Dave had regained his composure, and hearing it helped Stella to calm herself.

The tears stopped. She managed to get them off her eyes, but they were streaking down the sides of her helmet and visor.

At least it wasn't vomit.

It was the wrong thought. Sally immediately flashed into her mind, and fear flooded her again.

Stella took deep breaths, trying to remember her training. *Breathe deep, breathe calm.*

Slowly, as she listened to Dave and Zeld, the fear was forced down to the back of her mind.

"I've got you both on the map. I think I have that thing's heat signature following you."

"Why didn't you pick it up earlier?"

"I think the storm was interfering with the signal. It's still burning pretty hot out here."

"I've told you a million times about the sensors, Dave," Zeld said.

"You're right. I can't do anything about this now."

"You could not be a cheap-ass."

"Noted. Looks like you've got some time. You might be able to make it to the exit."

"That's too far back. Take me somewhere else."

Pause. Stella licked her lips, salty from her tears. Her body felt limp and empty.

She accepted her fate.

"I'll take you to the maintenance tunnels. Turn left, go down about twenty yards, and it should be inside the door to your right."

"Going."

"Stella, are you okay?"

The urge to wipe her face was too much, but she couldn't do anything about it now. "I'm here. I'm not okay."

"You've gone quite a ways into the ship. By the engine room, it looks like. Let me get you to Zeld and we'll get you both off."

"I don't want to," Stella whimpered. She hated herself for sounding so pitiful, and it almost set her back to crying.

"Stella? Will you trust me?"

The words threw her back.

Their hands entwined. The warmth of his skin on hers was delicious, and she rubbed her cheek against his chest. The smell of him was close, a hint of sweat, oil, and metal.

"We could do it again, you know. Just give me a few minutes."

She looked up into his eyes and smiled. He returned it, his eyes filled with warmth. She gave a quick little giggle, feeling giddiness rise from her toes to the top of her head.

"If you want. You haven't told me much about you?"

"Not much to tell."

"Oh?" She let go of his hand, tracing around his bellybutton. He rubbed her shoulder with a thumb absentmindedly. "What about where you grew up?"

"On a space miner out in the Centauri region."

"Picking up rocks? How was that?"

"No, we mined asteroids for methane. Quite lucrative, in the right markets." He took a deep breath and stared out of the small window into space. "It's been a while since I've thought about that."

Stella murmured, giving him the silence to continue. He didn't. "What about family?"

"Gone." His body tensed.

"Mine too."

He shifted and kissed her head. It helped stem the dark thoughts that were invading her mind. "I'm sorry to hear that."

"They died in an accident." If you could call it that. "Here one day and gone the next."

His heartbeat was calm, steady. Comforting. "What are we, Stella?"

She looked up at him, into those pained, questioning eyes.

"What do you mean?"

"There's so much swirling inside me. I feel mixed up." He looked away. "I... care for you. More than anyone else. I don't know why I feel this way, but I do."

A warm feeling ran up her body, in spite of her discomfort. "We are what we are. Don't overthink this." She let go of him, brought a hand to his cheek. His jaw was firm, his skin rough with stubble. Gently, she brought his face back to look at her. "I care about you too."

A flicker of a smile played on his face, then turned into a real one. It melted her heart. He was so beautiful when he smiled, all the way up to his eyes and beyond.

She couldn't help but return it, feeling warm and bubbly all over. "Will you trust me?"

He nodded.

"I'm here," Stella said. "I'm ready."

"You can do this," Dave said. "I'm going to be here to guide you."

She looked down the passage, tight and gray. It was dark, as black as space, except for where her light played along the walls and floor.

A tumble of pipes ran overhead, crammed just above her. She licked her lips, still salty, and sniffed. "What do I need to do?" she whispered.

She still fought the overwhelming urge to scramble farther into the corner, to hide and to run as fast as she could. Her heart pounded inside her chest.

A quick glance down to her display. She was running out of oxygen. And time.

"I'm going to keep you safe, keep you out of the way of that thing. Go back the way you came and turn left."

"Where is it?" Stella asked.

"It's in the outer ring of the ship. I can see it now."

She got back up to her shaky feet, grabbing onto the pipes above. There was still some residual gravity, she didn't know why.

With a quick click she disconnected her shoes from the floor, turning off her magnets.

Her body floated up, and she pushed gently off ahead of her.

"I can see you moving now," Dave said. "Good, keep going."

Her breathing had slowed, but still wasn't down to normal. She couldn't, not after what had happened. The stale smell of recycled air distracted her. Soon it would burn out of oxygen and be overcome with carbon dioxide.

Unless she made it back to the ship in time.

"My air is low."

"I can see it. I see both of your suits just fine. We have plenty of time to get you back to the *Beauty*, don't you worry." The calm was back in his voice, and was soothing. This was the Dave she remembered. Solid, dependable. No matter what happened.

Even when the job turned bad.

"Zeld, I'm going to have you turn left up ahead." Stella had almost forgotten she needed direction too. "Stella, you keep to the right for the next two turns. Speak up if you need anything."

She floated to the turn, her heart beating faster as she approached. Her mind flashed with imagination, thinking of what could be over there, just out of sight.

Something cutting through her neck went through her mind, paralyzing her. She tried to turn her head, see around the corner, but it was no use.

For a minute she wished she had a weapon, but then remembered the pistol on her belt. She took it out now, holding it in front of her with two shaking hands.

A light push sent her forward at a good speed. Dave was giving directions to Zeld, but her attention was wholly focused on getting around that corner.

A brief flash of light on the wall, then her light illuminated the tunnel. Empty.

She twisted, turned around to look the other way. Half of her expected a death blow at any second.

Also empty.

She sucked in a deep breath, holding out her hand to stop on the other side of the tunnel. Stella stopped for a few seconds, visions of death filling her mind.

How was she going to go forward?

"Stella, you have this." Dave's voice crackled in her ear, intimately close and quiet.

It helped, but didn't banish the fear. She pushed off again, slower than she would like.

The tunnel rushed by. She made the right, still feeling the terror rise as she approached.

It was easier this time, and there was no sign of anything but maintenance tunnel as far as her light illuminated.

"I've found the entrance," Zeld said. "Going inside now."

"Just in time. It's on the move."

Stella felt the back of her neck tingle, and her hair crawl. She looked behind her wildly, swinging her head around.

The movement threw her off balance, sending her careening into the wall. She hit hard enough to see stars, despite the helmet protecting her.

Her status flashed angry red, alarms blaring for a moment then cutting off. Her heartbeat flashed to an extreme pace, and her breathing matched it.

The fear was overwhelming her again. She thrashed out, hit the wall with her hands, the hardness of it hurting her hand.

"You're safe, Stella. Keep moving."

"I'll be seeing you in a few minutes," Zeld said. "And I expect a warm welcome."

The voices anchored her. She grabbed onto a pipe.

Her suit evened out, the alarms silencing as it worked to fix itself. One by one the warnings flashed away, except one.

Helmet integrity critical.

The alarm was off, but the bright red splash in the lower corner of her visor was impossible to miss. She felt at it, managing to trace a small web of cracks even through the glove.

"Are you hurt?" Dave asked. Of course he could see it on the ship.

"I'm fine." She took a deep breath, calming her heart. "Took a tumble, that's all."

"You only have a few more turns to go. Keep going, Stella," Dave said.

She moved, pushed off the wall and down the corridor. Even though she was afraid, terrified, she kept moving. Thinking of Dave kept her going, and the future.

Stella fixated on it. It helped to think about it, ignoring everything else except moving forward. She slipped into herself, listening only to the sound of Dave's directions, following them through the ship.

"Dave," Stella said. She wanted to continue, but couldn't find the words. The pipes trailed by her as she floated forward. Her heart pounded in her ears, each second feeling worse than the last. Something felt like it was constricting around her throat, but she knew nothing was there.

But she knew it would come.

If she didn't make it out in time.

"What is it, Stella?"

"I—" She swallowed. "I want you to know that I…"

"I know." He was so sure. How could he be so sure? "I do too." A pause. The sound of her breathing. "Left here."

She turned, and there it was. The access hatch to the exterior, livable portions of the ship. Why had they come here? *Why didn't we just stay away?*

"Is it?"

"Not next to you, at least. Not yet."

Something chirruped, then Zeld came in. "I've almost got it." It was a small moment of joy, but it was quickly squashed when Stella reached out and felt her grip close around the solid handle of the hatch door.

"Move faster, Zeld." Something skipped in her heart. Dave was outwardly calm, but something in his voice, ever so slight, made her pulse quicken. Her breathing was fast, too fast, and she tried to calm down.

Her hands trembled, clasped around the metal. She couldn't feel it through the gloves, but it would be ice-cold. The same temperature as space. The same temperature as her body would be once she—

No, don't *think of that!*

"Almost through now." It was Zeld, and something strange scraping or rasping against something else. Metallic. "One more turn."

"Stella, you need to leave now," Dave said.

But It was out there.

Right on the other side of that haze-gray door. Waiting for her like it had been for the others.

Her hands trembled, locked onto the hatch handle for dear life.

I have to go! I have to get out!

But her body wouldn't respond. It was frozen like the vastness of space. She was crying now, sobbing in her helmet. Voices chattered, but she couldn't hear them, not really.

Is this how you're going to die? Stella squeezed her eyes shut. The thick taste of tears rolled into her mouth. She would never see the beach, never taste the sunset again.

Something clicked then, deep inside her.

"Go, Zeld. Fast," Dave said. There was panic in his voice.

Somehow the words freed her hands as well. She shuddered, then her arms moved, straining against the overwhelming tension in the door. It resisted at first, fighting to keep her in, but Stella kept pulling.

It moved, breaking free. Then it jerked again, another inch more.

Once more.

Then, it was free.

She spun it faster now, faster and faster. The heavy panting of Zeld's breathing was in her ear through the static bursts of interference. The handle flew, and then stopped with a jolt.

Stella spun in the air, tucked her knees up to her chest, then kicked out with all her might.

Her feet struck, sending a shockwave up her body, sending her flying back into the tunnel. She scrambled, reached out, grabbed onto the pipes with the knuckles of two fingers, and slammed into the side of the tunnel.

And the door opened, smacking into the wall like a church bell tolling out for a funeral.

Blackness stared at her.

She knew she had to go out into the void, knew the only way to escape was that direction.

But there was something else out there too.

Lurking in the dark.

Something flashed. It could have been it.

Stella took a deep breath and, before she could second-guess herself, pushed off the wall and forward into the void. She closed her eyes as her body entered the empty hallway.

Any second she would feel it.

That thing cutting through her throat. The metallic or bone scythe would part her head from her body, just like it had done to the others.

A second passed, then another.

She was still alive, and Dave was calling for her in her ear. Stella opened her eyes, dread suffocating her, and she wildly looked around, her flashlight lancing through the blackness like a laser.

It wasn't here.

"Stella, go down the corridor to your right. And please, hurry." Dave was shaken, so unlike himself.

"I'll…" Her voice trailed off. "I'm going." Her voice came out a broken whisper in the blackness, consumed quickly into the reaches of space. The momentum had carried her to the far side of the hallway, within reach of the wall.

She reached out and grabbed a door handle, then used it to push herself to the right. She didn't want to make a sound, but the sound of her feet tapping against the metal echoed like alarms in the corridor. Her body glided through the spaceship, powered by hands and feet on the wall and the metallic deck beneath her.

She thought she caught a glimpse of something out of the corner of her eye and spun to the left. Her flashlight bounced wildly, but when it came to rest on the patch of darkness she had seen shifting, there was nothing. Heart racing, she tried to calm down.

A ragged breath caught in her throat and her hand went down to the pistol at her side. What she was going to do with it, she didn't know.

"Stella, keep going." Dave's voice crackled and broke in the silence of the tomb she found herself in. Had he seen her stop? Or was there something else he knew about?

Was it there? Right behind her?

Dread crept up her back, seeping into her muscles, freezing her everywhere. Her breath caught again. It felt like a giant hand was pressing against her chest. Her momentum was carrying her forward, her light trailing along the sterile, gray walls.

She wanted to turn and look behind her, but she couldn't. It would be there. Stella squeezed her eyes shut, wanting it all to be over and all to go away. Tears streamed silently down her cheek.

I have to keep going. Stella tried to think of something... better. She tried to picture Dave's face, the feel of his hand on her skin, the way he gave her goosebumps with that look in his eye.

She grabbed onto the side of the corridor. With a trembling hand she pushed off, propelling her towards the shaft of light illuminated by her headlamp.

And deeper into the ship.

She flew past floating pieces of debris, preserved artifacts from a time long since passed. A glove here, a tool there. There weren't many, but there were enough for her to feel the isolation, the touch of the past.

But she kept moving. She kept gliding forward into the corridor.

Her heartbeat pounded in her ear.

Inch by inch, foot by foot, she was traveling through the ship. Sometimes she glimpsed something that might be familiar, a hint of a hatch, strange symbols on the wall, all shaking free a hint of a memory in her dread-soaked mind, but never enough to latch onto.

And never enough to give her hope.

Her breathing came in quick, ragged bursts, each bringing with it the stale breath of recycled air. Every muscle in her body screamed at her, either from fear or from overuse.

"Turn right up at the next junction," Dave said. Calm had re-entered his voice, but not enough to cover over the slightest hint of fear. It was touching, to know that he still cared about her despite what she wanted.

Here she was, trying to get to the one place she didn't want to be.

Stella closed her eyes. She was floating alone, in space, like those poor, unfortunate souls they had come across. Their eyes, she remembered their eyes, and shuddered. The look of horror, the knowledge of destruction.

A taste of what she was feeling now.

A hint of what was to come.

She was sinking back down, the dread overcoming her. That feeling of something at her back was creeping up again, making the hairs on the back of her neck stand up on end like receiving dishes.

"Stella, turn right." Dave's voice brought her back from the brink. A tiny glimmer of hope of seeing him again fluttered in her chest.

She opened her eyes.

There was nothing in the corridor. Between heartbeats she repeated the words.

Nothing. There is nothing.

She turned right, gliding silently from a gentle push off the wall. The metal sucked the heat from her body. Her gloves didn't make a sound.

For that, she was grateful.

Every heartbeat was one second longer.

Every breath was one step closer.

She glided, led by Dave through the tomb of a ship. Her light flashed around corners. At each one she expected to see something.

At each one there was only silence, and that eerie stillness of death.

A quick glance at her display told her the air was running out even faster.

"Zeld, you're almost there. Just take a quick turn into that room up on your left," Dave said.

"I can make it."

"Trust me." There was a pause. The hair crept up Stella's neck, and to her horror, no small measure of relief.

"I'm in now."

"Lock the door. And stay silent. Stella, I've got you up for the next turn." The calm, steady Dave she knew and loved was back. The voice she had remembered through so many missions.

Even the last one.

She was still drifting through the ship, but something caught her attention as it passed into the circle of her light and then was gone.

That strange marking that reminded her of her childhood teddy bear.

A flash of hope burned in her.

She remembered.

"Stella, what's wrong?" She realized she had gasped, and now Dave was alarmed. Even across the distance it touched her heart, made it soft and supple.

"I know where I am now." She pushed off the nearest wall, accelerating down the corridor. Brushing off bits of flying debris, she urged herself on.

"Good, you're almost there."

There were only a few more turns left to the airlock. Only a few more feet to freedom.

Her breathing echoed in her ears, each one another sip of oxygen so precious it was painful. She thought something moved up ahead, and jerked her light over to it.

A glove drifted into the corridor.

A chill ran down her spine, and she almost threw up.

It wasn't empty. Droplets floated behind it and she altered course to avoid it.

She sucked in a deep breath of air, then squeezed her eyes shut. That glove was too familiar.

"Just keep going," she told herself, grateful to hear the sound of her own voice.

Another turn was coming up ahead. She had to open her eyes.

She did.

Blinking, she took a second to reorient herself. Blood pounded in her ears, her heart running overtime. For a second she was lost, and almost called out to Dave. Panic clawed at her.

Then, she recognized the door up ahead, and she was suddenly back in a familiar, if not strange, place. The same cold, gray metal. The same red sign at the lower right.

Stella stopped a moment to rest and push back the fear. Her hands trembled worse than coming out of hyperspace. As she calmed her breathing she wondered why she hadn't heard Dave or Zeld. How long had it been?

The clock on her helmet display told her only a few minutes had passed, ten at most.

And her oxygen levels were critical. At this rate she would have little time to make it to the ship. Worry pulled at her at the lack of communication.

I'm overthinking this. Still, she patted the hefty weight of the pistol at her hip. For not the first time she regretted not taking up Andy's offer to teach her better marksmanship.

It might have come in handy.

"Dave, I'm almost there," she said.

Silence.

Stella gnawed on her bottom lip and hesitated. Something wasn't right, she could feel it in the pit of her stomach. Nothing more could be done than to get out, though, and Stella pushed off, regaining her course.

A few turns later the airlock hatch flashed into view, glowing like a beacon calling her home. Her entire body, tense with fright, relaxed just a hair. Outside, the deep cold of space beckoned, stars burning bright and solid.

The wheel of the airlock felt solid under her hands. "I'm at the airlock." She turned it, and it gave little resistance before spinning silently in the dead space.

Dave should have responded. By the time the wheel clicked open, she knew something was wrong.

"Dave, what is it?" Nothing.

"Zeld, come in." Quiet. "Can anyone hear me?"

Stella tugged. The oversized airlock hatch slipped off its face, the hinges creaking. The quiet sound screamed through her helmet, and she jerked her head left and right down the corridor.

"Dave, what's going on?" Her transponder seemed to be working, but even her suit batteries were alarming now. Dangerous thoughts flew through her head. Only the worst outcomes that ended in death materialized.

"I'm at the airlock." Dave's voice was solid, but cold. All the warmth was gone. A quick glance outside was all it took to confirm the comforting sight of *Black Beauty*.

Stella's heart dropped. Then she realized what had sent cold spines of ice up her back. He had tried to hide it, but she had picked it out.

She was out of time.

"Dave," she pleaded. Mechanisms clicked and moved. *Black Beauty* was on the other side of the hatch, just waiting for her.

A place of comfort, a place of home.

But it was so far away it felt like it was on the other side of the galaxy.

Stella didn't want to look behind her. Dread piled up like a mass of antimatter to consume her. She pushed open the hatch and entered the airlock.

Her breath came in short bursts as she spun.

"Don't look," Dave said.

But it was too late.

Her arms began to twitch uncontrollably and the strength went out of her legs.

"Dave."

It was there.

"Shut the hatch." There was too much fear and urgency in his voice.

It wasn't supposed to be here. She couldn't move.

"Stella, SHUT THE HATCH!"

His voice spurred her into action.

She pushed, scrambling as her body found nothing but space to push against. Legs flailed as it approached.

Her heartbeat pounded in her ear. Time seemed to slow.

All sense of hearing was gone.

Just a single, solitary tone ringing in her ears.

Her entire body was shaking.

IT was getting closer.

Her leg struck the wall of the airlock. A jolt ran down her leg up into her body.

It struck her, pulled her out of paralysis.

Stella turned and planted both feet on the wall and pushed with all her might.

Her breath caught in her throat, her legs screaming, the hatch inched shut. The door might buy time.

Might.

One second passed.

One heartbeat.

Another.

Two more.

The thing dripped blood from deadly fangs.

The hatch sped up, her heart pounding.

It was shutting.

Another heartbeat.

Was this how it was going to end? Stella shut her eyes. She floated on the hatch.

Funny, I always heard your life flashed before your eyes.

Her body wrenched as the hatch struck. Her heart was pounding, her breath drawn in ragged gasps.

The oxygen alarm screamed at her, the high pitch in her ears.

Stella gripped the hard handle of the hatch wheel and planted her feet, clicking on the magnets. She spun it shut just as something, it, slammed into the hatch.

The hatch wheel stopped. Stella pulled out the pistol at her belt and struck it.

It clicked into place.

"Stella!" Dave was shouting in her ear, broken by static or interference, or something. Her vision was clouded, her mind in a haze as she turned.

The airlock was open. Dave's arms slipped around her waist.

Another *thunk*, a toll of death behind them.

Then, she was moving through the hatch. Dave's face was framed in light as a steady fog of black pulled around him.

The fog closed in. The last thing she saw was his face.

"There you are." Hands in her hair, caressing her. "I'm glad you came back," Dave said, his voice cracking. Long, thin lines tensed at the corners of his eyes, and his smile was too... forced.

Stella took a deep breath as she came out of unconsciousness, breathing in the sterile, comforting smell of the scrubbers. The ship beeped and hummed, vibrating her in a gentle hug.

It was overwhelming.

Hot tears sprung at her eyes. Her hands clutched at Dave and he pulled her into a suffocating embrace. The cool of the metal surgical table touched her exposed legs.

He was crying too. Gentle sobs that wracked his body, as if he were trying to hold it back and couldn't.

It broke all her inhibitions and all the emotions she had pent up the last few hours rushed out. She cried until her body was left shaking.

"Zeld?" His head shook against her shoulder. Her body let out an involuntary wail. More tears flowed.

Tears of grief. Tears of relief.

Tears of guilt that she had made it out alive when no other did.

They were all gone. It was hard to believe. Everything flowed out.

Just like that mother and child she found clutched in each other's embrace. *Will there be a salvager to find our bodies like we found theirs?*

Slowly her tears dried up. Dave's heartbeat in her ear as he held her tight.

"Are we... safe?"

Dave nodded. "I booked it out of there as fast as I could." His pause made her breath short. "It was still inside the ship."

"Good." The dread that had filled her at the thought of that thing stalking them on their own ship subsided. Stella tried to stand up on shaky legs, but couldn't support her own weight.

Dave caught her.

"Take it slow. Sit down. Here." He threw a blanket over her shoulders and rubbed her arms. "You're as cold as space."

"Where do we go from here, Dave?" The words came out in a barely perceptible whisper. His eyes stared into hers, bright pools of color in the drab gray surroundings.

At once she hated it all. The life in space, the sterility of it all.

She wanted to escape.

But to where?

"I don't know, Stella. I don't know."

He kissed her. The warmth and passion overtook her.

The blanket slipped off her shoulders as she reached up and touched him, touched a living creature of flesh and blood. Touched someone she cared deeply for.

Not just care, love.

For a moment she forgot everything. The bliss of love overtook her.

Eclectic Stories

Thank you for spending your precious time reading this book.

If stories make you salivate, learn more about lore, take an exclusive sneak peek behind the scenes, and get writing updates in my newsletter, Eric's Eclectic Stories.

As a bonus you'll get *Stories from the Deep*, a Patmos Sea Fantasy Adventure anthology that gives a glimpses of lore, extra prologues and epilogues, and character backstories.

If you aren't satisfied, unsubscribe at any time.

Join at erickercher.com.

-Eric Kercher

Also By Eric Kercher

Patmos Sea Fantasy Adventure Series

Fathomless Pursuit - Architect's Prize - Ironbound Path
Sunken Prey – Unanswered Prophecy – Hardened Pilgrim – Final
Peace

Seventh Hall Chronicles

Seventh Hall - Ode to the Survivors - Bastion of the Deep

Epic of Hornblood Castle

Siege of the Unfinished Keep – Winter at Hornblood – Branch of the
Everlong

Castlebound Adventures

Rats in the Cellar!- Save the Cat!

Collections

Red Eagle Anthology | Searchlight Anthology

Stand Alone

Planet Reaping | Dukedom Rumble | Savage Space Salvage

About Author

Eric Kercher was born and raised in a small town on the Great Plains on good books. After attending a small state school on the east coast he joined the US Navy to serve his country and explore the world. He worked on submarines, and the world beneath the waves captivated him with all its mysteries and wonders. After spending time in larger cities, he's settled down in a quiet town with his wife and children. When not on an adventure in a good book the author enjoys creating dust woodworking, architecture, and spending time with loved ones.

Find out more at www.erickercher.com.